Nighttime, Bedtime
Stories for Children

By

Diana Olson

ISBN: 0-7596-2993-5

This book is printed on acid free paper.

1stBooks - rev. 1/10/02

Deanna The Mystical Ballerina.

There once lived a mystical ballerina, named Deanna.

She lived in two worlds, A part of her world was a kingdom.

The other part of her world was mystical!

There were people called nobles, They lived in the blackhills.

Diana Olson

They had escaped from King Richards of the kingdom of the greens, because they were in non-payment of there taxes.

7

Diana Olson

They were trying to take over King Richards thrown but when they threaten to fight King Richards and his honored people of the kingdom of the greens.

Something very mystical would happen Deanna
the ballerina!

She would turn into a black cougar and scare them away!

Deanna was defiantly special!

When King Richards would have celebrations,
King Richards would always send for Deanna the
mystical ballerina in a carriage.

Deanna even seemed to light shinny stars!

She would make them a little bit brighter.

When she danced for King Richards and the
Kingdom of the greens.

King Richards was unwedded and looking for a
bride.

Oh how the ballerina longed for him.

One rain storm day King Richards called, For his carriage, and his horsemen to take him to the valley of the sun's arising!

Where he loved to fish!

The ballerina Deanna happen to be there.

They took glances at each other, They fell in-love.

Suddenly Deanna leaves in a storm.

Diana Olson

Then King Richards is captured by the nobles of
the black hills.

King Richards was gone for days days became
weeks!

Deanna became worried so!

The people of the Kingdom of the greens worried and talked where could King Richards be?

Then shiny stars shined over Deanna.

She had remembered about the nobles fighting
with King Richards.

Deanna used her mystical powers and turned into a
black cougar.

Diana Olson

She jumped valleys, she jumped mountains.

32

Until she found King Richards tied around a tree!

She pulled the horsemen to King Richards to save King Richards!

King Richards was dazed!

King Richards and the Kingdom of the greens
arrested the nobles of the blackhills!

They put them in a cell!

Diana Olson

Then King Richards called for a celebration and
sent for Deanna the mystical ballerina.

She then came into the ballroom in pink and white.

The stars were then brighter.

Once again she danced with King Richards.

He asked for her hand in marriage.

She said yes!

They lived happily in the Kingdom of the greens
forever!

Written by Diana L. Olson

This story is about , A love friendship between two
different animal's named Taria and Elfrado.

The forest of the Eclipse.

A rabbit named, Taria loved a frog named, Elfardo.

Well as the story goes they both loved each other, but because they were so diffrent: The forest of the Eclipse didn't agree with there friendship!

Diana Olson

The other forest creatures didn't like them and
began to through sticks at them!

They had ran them out of the forest of the Eclipse!

Taria and Elfardo had met friends along the way.

On there journey into the high mountains they met a pumkin who would leave a lite on because part of the forest was dark! and very gloomy.

Winter was comming around and The pumkin lite there way to a log and some leaves for his friends Taria and Elfardo.

They were sad that the other creatures didn't approve of there friendship: For instance: Brilly the bangle bear, and Faria the rhinoceros , Eddie the singing zebra.

There was nosseta the nosy stick throwing elephant!

Well taria and Elfardo ment some friends along the way named Zachary the barefoot bear! and Sammy the toothless tiger.

There was pucky the colorful pheasant!

They sang songs together.

Diana Olson

They laughed and played games together like hide
and seek!

One sunny go lucky day Elfrado fell down a hill he bumped his head on a rock!

A mystical fly cast a spell over Elfardo: "he became strong".

He Awoke, The mystical fly whispered to Elfardo:
King Frankie of the forest of the Eclipse was in
trouble!

Diana Olson

A log has rolled over King Frankie leggs for he was a giraffe.

Elfardo and Taria and there friends from the high mountains came to help King Frankie by rolling the log off him.

Diana Olson

The forest of the Eclipse clapped together.

King Frankie granted Taria and Elfardo back into
the Forest of the Eclipse.

Suddenly! in amazement The Eclipse comes out!

The other creatures had apologized to Taria and Elfardo.

King Frankie gave a log and laid it into the crystal pond for Taria and Elfardo. "They beamed at each other.

They lived happily forever in the Forest of the Eclipse!

Written by Diana L Olson

Diana Olson

Sammy The Chinese Clock.

Sammy Was A Chinese Clock.

Diana Olson

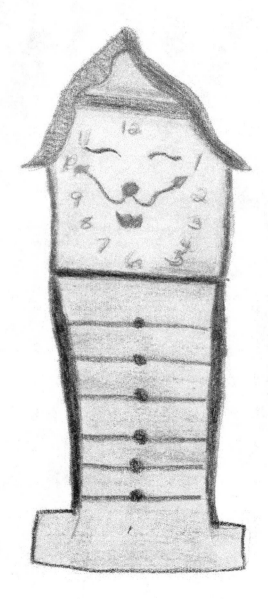

He Came all the way from the Great Wall.

A couple named: Sara and Joseph took good care of Sammy.

They were religious leaders.

They traveled to Samara China on a ship.

There was something special about Sammy!
Sammy was sacred: He had hidden treasures inside
a drawer.

When anyone would come near Sammy and his treasures "He would sneeze!" and Loudly!

To scare off unwanted criminals away.

One day the zoo-Lou wrestlers came to visit
Joseph and Sara for tea and crumpets.

They were impressed with Sammy!

They asked, "Sara and Joseph to buy Sammy?"

Joseph replied: Under no circumstances must the Chinese clocks leave my premises, Sara replied: "As religious Leaders it is our duty to care for Sammy the Chinese clock", It has been our history!

The zoo-Lou wrestlers left: Then a few weeks
went by it had been a full moon coming out!

Sara had made her full moon orange cakes it was culture for her to bake.

Joseph had decided take Sara to the full moon
parades they left: Who would have been watching
but the zoo-Lou wrestlers!

They watched Sara and Joseph leave!

They bounced there bellies into the door, "They went! Stumbling and rolled on top of one another!

One zoo-Lou wrestler had stumped his toe! (Who-he!) (Who-he!) He exclaimed.

Diana Olson

There were three zoo-Lou wrestler's there names were Gusta, Whitener, and sinaria.

They were the clumsiest zoo-Lou wrestlers and criminlists! Whoever knew: "The Simmaria police! department.

They pulled on Sammys hidden treasures and took pieces of jewelry. The dumbest criminals in zoo-Lou wrestlers stumbled around. Until the sirens went off!

Sammy was sneezing loudly on and on! Then the Simmaria police came into the house and arrested the zoo-Lou wrestlers.

Sara and Joseph the religious leaders came home.

They said: It certainly has been a full moon tonight!

Diana Olson

Nothing was taken from Sammy the clock.Sara and Joseph looked up at the full moon with their orange pound cake as the fog started to cover it up.

Written by Diana L Olson
On December 28, 1995

The little Pariates Parade.

Peter, a boy who livedvery long ago, was playing pirate all the time. He would always put a patch over his eye and wear a red bandanna. His father had his own sailboat.

Peter would find himself constanly playing on the boatas if he was captain of a pirate's ship. Peter's parents thought he was being silly. On top of that, Peter had to deal with his

Diana Olson

Friends who would laugh at him! Billy, the main cause of stress for young Peter, laughed at him one day because he was always playing the pirate. Billy sneered and poked fun at

Peter by stating, "have you found any buried treasure yet!" Tommy, one of Billy's buddies exclaimed as he fell to the ground laughing his head off, "Ha! Ha! Ha! Ha!" Peter was very

Embarrassed by the actions of Billy and Tommy that he said that he would get even with them someday. On a windy, rainy, and gloomy fall day, the orange and yellow leaves

Began to fall. While Peter was walking home, he tripped over a pile of leaves! He immediately fell to the ground and became unconscience. Tommy had walking by and notice Peter hurt. Fortunately, Peter always carried the pirate bandanna on him. Tommy placed it on the soar to help Peter get better. Suddenly, Billy who was lookng for his

friends Tommy, seen Peter laying on this sidewalk
and they stopped to help. Billy and

Tommy ran to Peter's home and screamed to his parents, "Help Peter, he is unconscience

on the sidewalk." Peter's mother called the
hospital and they sent the ambulance. After

which seemed like a long wait the ambulance
finally arrived. Meanwhile, Peter is having a

dizzy spell and dreaming of his buried treasure. As he dreamed, he was on a ship on the

Diana Olson

ocean side of Columbia. The ships captain Juilus a
older man with black grey hair and

beard, "He wore black boots and jewlery that he had found in treasure's under the sea."

as he told young Peter there was a time the storms
were so teriffing that he did everything

to save his crew and his treasure's. As darkness
became the night the ship was rocking

Diana Olson

softly, as the crew slept captian Juilus doesed off
snoring loudly. The waves began to

bigger and bigger. The thunder roared! The lightning Zig-Zaged in the sky shooting down

like a falling star onto the Island. As the wind
picked up the ships crew was still sleeping

one crew member named, "Pounce" woke up to
Captian Julius snoring! And the seas roar

as so did Peter. Pirate Pounce told Peter, "Peter quickly grabb the stirring wheel! Peter

did just that he started stirring the ship. Pounce
yells the crew on deck to awaken at once.

Pounce went aboard the ship and grabbed a rope to stir the ship. Suddenly water splashes

onto Captian Julius getting him wet! He grumbles
and shacks his head and beard. He

open one eye and then the other seeing Peter
stirring the wheel of the ship as the storm

grummbled! As the waves hit the ship Peter would
hang on. Captain Julius would guild

Peter for he had a missing leg and the storm was to
much for him as he could'nt do

anything else. Peter stirred the ship back to calm seasand as it passed captian Julius

clapped for Peter and so did the crew! Peter relized
that being a pirate is of hardship and

stormming seas. As he awoken to say, "Lets have a treasure's day pirates parade"! Peter's mother whiper's "I love you honey". Peter finaly came around, and everyone was happy!

The doctor's said to Peter, "We were worried about you. Then everyone else said we

were to! Tommy said to Peter, "What were you
talking about Peter do you remember?

Peter exclaimed "Lets have a Pirates Parade!"
They all agreed, by the way Peter your

bandanna came in handy with your soar said,
Tommy. Tommy said to Peter, I'm sorry

Peter I teased you about your pirate spirit. Billy said I'm espeially sorry Peter. The parents of Peter asked them if they learned a lesson. The children looked at each other in a sign.

The next week they planned the pirates parade.
Peter's parents dressed their boat to the

way of the pirate. They all had canes like Captian
hook. On the day of the pirat's parade,

thay blew whistles and dressed up in pirate's cosumes which their mothers had made for

them with black patchs over their eyes. They sang
songs and Peter held his cane with the

red bandanna on it The children marched to his
father's newly formed pirate sailboat and

they waved to everyone!

The End.

Written by Diana Lynn Olson
September 13, 1998.

Troop 22 at Fire Engine School.

Charlie was a boy of three.

He had a brother named, Joey, they had a friend
named, Sonny.

There Moms were troop Leaders They decided to bring troop 22 to have a day at fire engine school.

It would be held at district 56 fire station.

It was held on Saturday at 11:00 AM.

Fire chief Stubby and his teaching crew would
await troop 22.

Mrs. Lightfoot a cub scout leader and Mrs. Olaf loaded up the cub scouts in there stationwagon.

Diana Olson

Mrs. Olaf said, Children fellow cub scouts of troop 22.

This will help you earn a bange.

Fire Chief Stubby put fire hats on all the cub
scouts and fire jackets.

157

Diana Olson

Charlie the three years sold wad excited, He got to wear a fire hat Chief Stubby asked his teaching crew to put the children on the fire truck and began telling the children Never play with matches!

He exclaimed, how important it is not to smoke cigarettes because they can also start fires.

As he explained, also you must know to always dial 9-11 if they should smell or see smoke around.

Troop 22 got ice-cream at the end of the day.

The cubs scouts said, goodbye.

The troop leaders of troop 22 thanked Chief stubby and his teaching crew.

Diana Olson

They all got into the stationwagon and rode away
in the sunset.

Everyone at the district 56 waved.

Written by Diana L Olson
February 28, 1999

Diana Olson

Diana Olson

ABOUT THE AUTHOR

I enjoy the pleasure writing gives me, and I hope maybe some positives can come from reading these short stories. I work as a Dietetic Assistant in a hospital, and I have two sons. I love to write.

CPSIA information can be obtained
at www.ICGtesting.com
Printed in the USA
BVHW082140100222
628623BV00004B/621